Publication design by zzGassman design workshop

Artwork by Nicole Handel

Logo design by Nelle Dunlap

The excerpt from *Eyelid Lick* is printed here with permission from FENCE Books.

# Acknowledgments

# draft

The Journal of Process

Published by *draft journal*
5 Everett St., #1
Cambridge, MA 02138
www.draftjournal.com
ISBN #: 978-0-9853744-0-2

Artwork by: Nicole Handel
    "BBQ"
    30"x 40"
    Watercolor and Sharpie on Paper
    2011
Publication design by: zzGassman design workshop

Printed in the United States of America

# Contents

Alicia Erian    **Standing Up To The Superpowers**

Donald Dunbar    **Excerpt from *Eyelid Lick***

draft: ISSUE 2

# About *draft*

## The Journal of Process

*draft* publishes two issues per year, in the spring and fall. We are happy to provide creative writing teachers with desk copies upon request.

For information about future issues, subscriptions and purchasing, exercises for the classroom, suggestions, questions, or to get involved, please:

VISIT US ONLINE

www.draftjournal.com
facebook.com/draftjournal
@draftjournal on twitter

EMAIL

draftjournal@gmail.com

POST

the editors
*draft journal*
5 Everett St., #1
Cambridge, MA 02138

# From the Editors

The second issue has arrived! And it's full of firsts.

We are very excited to include our first poet, Donald Dunbar, whose first book won the 2012 FENCE Modern Poets Book Prize and will be published this fall by FENCE books. At the Association of Writers and Writing Programs Conference in Washington DC and Chicago, many readers asked if we would feature work outside of short fiction, and we answered with a selection of early drafts and final drafts of poems from Dunbar's forthcoming *Eyelid Lick*.

Another first comes in the interview with Dunbar—a nod to the benefits of LSD. The interview is exciting, because the poet is so candid and thoughtful, uncovering some of the most mysterious processes of generating, revising, and crafting a series of poems. Whether you are working on a novel, short story, play, poem, or memoir, this poet's advice on writing is helpful and liberating.

We're also featuring the first story from Alicia Erian's exquisite collection, *The Brutal Language of Love*. You might know Erian for her novel *Towelhead*, which was turned into a movie in 2007, directed by Alan Bell. We were alerted to her short stories by the always fabulous Roxane Gay, and we're so glad we were. Erian's stories combine dark wit, surprising characters and a lot of heart in a collection that's unforgettable. *Standing Up To The Superpowers*, in this issue, will probably wind up being one of your new favorite stories, as it has for us.

And finally, *draft* is featuring writing exercises submitted by our readers for the first time in this issue. Writing teachers and students (and all writers, really) use exercises to get their creative brain working, generating ideas, thinking in new ways, getting out of ruts. And we hope to cull the best exercises from our audience and provide them in each of our issues as well as on on our website, where we'll also be posting a few more exercises.

And so, without further ado, we give you Issue 2. Thanks, as ever, for reading.

Mark Polanzak          Rachel Yoder
Editors

# Alicia Erian

## Standing Up To The Superpowers

DRAFT — FINAL

# DRAFT

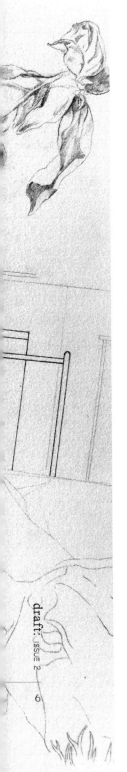

She passed out and he made love with her anyway. He was a vision and before she had passed out they had agreed on sex. He was drunk too and certain that he did have permission, and also that he couldn't wait. Afterward he felt terrible as he suspected he would. In the morning, when she woke up, he explained to her that he had raped her and asked her to drive him to the police state so he could turn himself in. She was irritated but said it was her fault for partying with a freshman. She turned himself in anyway but was sent home when the sophomore refused to press charges.

He had never felt so ashamed in all his life. He called his father who had always been so critical but who now seemed only willing to sympathize, saying that women could be very confusing and that he should know since had lost so many of them. Brian called his mom to see if she might be more willing to punish him. But since she had not had sex since she left Shipley's father, that angle embarrassed her. As a doctor, she felt more comfortable suggesting a morning after pill for the sophomore and perhaps counseling for Shipley if he was having some sort of dating problem.

He sat naked in his off campus apartment, staring at his violent penis. He couldn't imagine wanting to touch it for several weeks and so when he called the sophomore to suggest the morning after pill, she said she was already on birth control pills and he should leave her alone. He offered to get an AIDS test and she responded that unless he had been lying about being a virgin, she wasn't worried. He paused for a moment before asking her if she thought she should get and AIDS test, and she hung up on him. It had been an idiotic thing to say but he went and got a test anyway. If was negative but he appreciated the stress of having to await the result and the woman who told him he should come back in six months for another one. At least it was something.

A few months later he saw the sophomore walking down the street pregnant. He stopped and asked her if she remembered him and she said no. He knew she was lying and asked if the baby was his. She wondered how this was possible since she didn't know him and he begged her to stop fooling around.

They stopped at a café and had a drink. She said that it was probably his but that it could've been any body elses—they'd have to take a blood test. He apologized and she said for what? He asked why she hadn't take the morning after pill and she said the same thing.

# Final

Beatrice told Shipley she would sleep with him, and then she passed out. When she awoke the next morning, he said he'd gone ahead without her. He got dressed and asked her to drive him to the police station so he could turn himself in for rape, but she said not to worry about it. She wasn't happy, she said, but it was her own fault for drinking with a freshman. Shipley walked to the police station and turned himself in anyway. A Lieutenant Verbena called to see if Beatrice wanted to press charges and she said no. "Put him on," Beatrice said, and when Shipley said hello she hung up.

He called her the next day to say his mother, a pediatrician, had suggested she take a morning-after pill. "You told your mother?" Beatrice asked.

"She's a doctor," Shipley said.

"I got that."

"I'm going into counseling for my drinking," he added.

"How old are you?"

"Eighteen."

"I'm twenty-two," she said. "Now leave me alone."

Beatrice was a junior. She had taken a year off from college to work in a cheap clothing store for older women, then returned to school when she realized she made more money living off student loans. Her father, a divorce lawyer who had successfully represented himself against Beatrice's mother, had promised to help with tuition as long as Beatrice did well in high school. When she turned out to be not quite as smart as early test scores had indicated, however, he reneged. His advice to her was to stay away from the humanities, where there were no jobs.

She signed up for a Russian literature course with a professor named Fetko, who gave her good marks for implying that she'd be willing to sleep with him. Sometimes in his office he'd let her sip from his vending machine coffee, or take bites from the sandwiches his wife had prepared for him. Other times he gave her quarters for her own snacks. Mostly they just sat around shooting the shit, talking about Chekhov and his famous hemorrhoids. Shipley, the freshman, was also in Russian literature. Fetko hated him and so did Beatrice. He was always asking stupid questions

She stayed home alone every day. Her husband worked and she thought this was the way he wanted it. The first time she got bored she got a cat. The second time she got another cat. She had two cats and a computer game she liked a lot, but was still bored.

She had come from a poor family and was now well-to-do. She and her husband owned a two-level apartment in Manhattan with six bedrooms, a fireplace, and a piano which neither of them played but which was appreciated by visiting friends who had not come from poverty but rather apartments of similar size and music lessons. She talked openly with her friends about her origins, referring humorously to herself as noveau riche. The fact that she seemed to know her place only made it more difficult for her friends to find the differences between them.

She had come from truckers, cake decorators, factory workers, ad telephone operators, which her husband found to be humorous. "Imagine if they came to our house!" he would say not because he was a terrible snob but because he just couldn't imagine it.

She, however, was a terrible snob. She had become one when she'd seen the effect it had on her family, how it repulsed them and kept them away. She was angry with them, not for their poverty but for their belief that ~~wanting more was bad~~ noticing if you happened to get more was bad. They never had not relayed the story of a man who had won the lottery and acted as if his new mania was as baffling to him as it was to everyone else. "Money didn't change him one bit," her mother said.

Her mother called one day with a favor. "Kenneth needs a place to stay in New York. He was kidnapped that time — remember? And now he wants to write a book about it. He needs a place to stay and a computer. Can you help him?"
"Kenny?" she said
"He goes by Kenneth."
"Oh."
"He needs a place to stay."
"Uh-huh."
"You couldn't put him up for a few days?"
"He's going to write a book in a few days?"
"He's going to start writing the book while he looks for his own place," she said. She was starting to get irritated. It was her sister's kid and she wanted to look good to her sister.
"ok."

They exchanged phone numbers and she promised to call him when the baby was born.
It was a boy.

Shipley called the next day to ask about the morning after pill. She was

and interrupting Fetko's flow, something that was very important to Fetko. "Get him drunk and fuck with his head," Fetko had instructed Beatrice. "That would be worth a letter grade to me." Now, as she sat before her professor after Monday's class, Beatrice was unsure of what to say. "I fucked with him," she began, but when she described exactly how, Fetko turned white. "Jesus, Beatrice," he said, letting his pipe hang limp from his mouth.

She shrugged. She had been asleep when it happened.

—

Shipley called that afternoon to ask about the morning-after pill. Beatrice was sitting in her attic bedroom in a house filled with students. She had slept with two film majors on the second floor, one of whom had gone to great lengths to explain his uncircumcised penis to her. This had made her laugh--something she rarely did--and lose all interest in him, though she let him screw her anyway. "You're so hot," he'd whispered in her ear. "All the guys in the house want you."

"Thanks," she'd said, waiting for him to finish. Compliments had stopped doing it for her a long time ago.

Today she was trying to read a book about China for a history class. The professor was old and deaf, and whenever she tried to make a pass at him, he'd bellow, "What?" It was a grade she would actually have to work for, and it was killing her. Sometimes she went to his office to tell him this and he just nodded, pretending he could hear. She was no dummy. Her brain had just stopped accepting academic text along with the compliments.

What kind of name was Shipley anyway? Beatrice had half a mind to ask him now that he was on the phone, but didn't like to encourage friendship. Anyway, she was irritated, sick of his mother and this morning-after crap. "Don't worry about it," she told him. "I'm on birth control."

"What kind?" he asked, panting a little.

"What do you mean what kind?"

"What brand?"

"I don't know."

"Generic is cheaper."

"Fuck off."

sitting in her attic bedroom, trying to read a book about China.

see interview
question III,
page 32

"Don't worry about it," she told him. "I'm on birth control."

~~"My mother says I need to take responsibility."~~

"What kind?"

"What do you mean, what kind?"

"What brand?"

"I don't know."

"Generic is cheaper."

"Fuck off."

He laughed. "You have a nice personality. I liked you even before we got drunk."

"Thanks."

"You wanna keep talking?"

"Let me think. No."

"Can I call you again?"

"No."

"Can I talk to you in class?"

"No."

"After class?"

She hung up on him. He was in the love with her, that much was clear. It happened to her all the time. People were always falling in love with her, telling her she had a nice personality. Not all nice. Nice honest. She had stumbled on her personality quite by mistake, actually through her commitment to her depression. She believed she cared about nothing except her student loans. She loved no one in return. She had a fair amount of sex but it general preferred her own company and occasionally others. She was glad he never took her up on her offer for sex – just like the sound of the words coming out of her mouth because she felt it could weaken their friendship and she believed they had a sort of one. If she stopped talking dirty he would be disappointed but not punish her. People traded on what they had.

3

In class on Wednesday, Fetko seemed distracted. When Shipley raised his hand and asked Fetko to describe the socioeconomic conditions of the woman with the pet dog, he did without protest. Later, when Beatrice went to meet him in his office, he wasn't there. A note on his door said office hours were cancelled for the rest of the week.

Beatrice hoped Fetko's guilt wouldn't jeopardize their arrangement. She suffered brief anxiety over actually having to complete her assignments before purchasing her lunch from a vending machine and settling herself on a bench outdoors. Moments later Shipley joined her. He presented her with a card which read, "Sorry I raped you" inside.

4

"It's not funny, you know," she said, handing him the card back.

He took it. "I know."

"Then what the hell is this?"

"My parents think I should try to make it up to you."

He laughed. "You have a nice personality. I liked you even before we got drunk."

"Thanks."

"You wanna keep talking?"

"Let me think. No."

"I tried to talk to you after class today but you left so fast I couldn't find you."

"Try to   breathe slower," Beatrice instructed him.

"Can I talk to you after class on Wednesday?"

"No."

"Before class?"

She hung up on him. He was in love with her, that much was clear. It happened all the time; men loved her personality, thought it was nice. Not nice-nice obviously, but nice-honest. Back home, people said she was like her mother, who was often described as acidic, and who had become a lesbian after Beatrice left for college. "Sex is sex," she had once advised her daughter. "No need to be picky." What bothered Beatrice was her mother's refusal to come out in the liberal, northwestern city where she lived, instead preferring to divulge the intimate details of her love life solely to Beatrice, over the telephone.

"I don't want to hear it, Mom," Beatrice would say, at which point her mother would accuse her of being homophobic. Beatrice protested, saying she had never felt comfortable with her mother's bedroom stories about her father either. "So I guess I'll kill myself," was her mother's response, "if my own daughter won't even talk to me." It was Beatrice's freshman year and she didn't need the responsibility, so she listened. She allowed herself to be lost track of as a sophomore, however, moving off-campus and delisting her number. There was some comfort in knowing that neither of her parents had ever been of a mind to chase after her.

Increasingly, Beatrice loved no one. She had a fair amount of sex but in general preferred her own company, and on occasion that of Fetko. He had information about dead writers that fascinated her, health problems and such. She told him that after he died, people would say he had liked for his girl students to talk dirty to him, but he said no one would care since he wasn't a real writer. She pointed out his books of criticism and he told her she was sweet to be so naive, to have such big tits. In the end, though, she was glad he never tried to touch them, that it never

"Are you retarded or something?"

"I'm in college," he offered.

"You have some sort of emotional retardation, some freakishness in that way."

He shrugged. Briefly, a strange concern that she had hurt his feelings passed over her.

"Well," she said. "I'll take the card back, I guess."

"You're my first," he said.

"Is that right?" she said. She'd had many, many firsts.

"That's why you're kind of special to me."

"Uh-huh," she said.

"I'd like to introduce you to my parents," he said hopefully.

"You're a nice kid, "she said. "I don't really like to meet people's parents."

"My mother feeds expired birth control pills to her plants to fertilize them," he went on.

"Stop talking about that."

"Sorry," he said.

Fetko seemed back to his normal self on Friday. He refused to answer Shipley when…and was in his office after class. But when Beatrice said, "What time does your wife expect you home?" he stared back at her blankly. "Beatrice," he said, rubbing his eyes. "I've made a mistake here. We can talk as much as you want – anytime you want, but not about the stuff we used to talk about. And you need to start doing better on your quizzes."

She left his office stunned. She went home and masturbated, then fell asleep. Shipley called at about eleven pm.

"What do you want?" she said.

"I'm hoping we're going to make love again sometime. When you're awake."

"Forget it."

"What's the matter?" he said.

"My boyfriend dumped me," she said.

"You had a boyfriend?"

"Sort of."

"Wow." He paused. "Well that great that he dumped you. Now I have a better chance."

She laughed unexpectedly, something she hadn't done in weeks. "I guess you do."

"Really?" he said, excited.

She woke up more. "No."

She hung up in great spirits. She said she might be dropping out of college. He said his mother had offered to supply her with free birth control if she'd come over for dinner. She reasoned that her financial aid might not last that much longer, and accepted.

"What are your parents like?" he asked.

"I don't know," she said.

"They must be really special to have raised you."

went beyond talk. This would have weakened their rapport, which was something she felt they definitely enjoyed. Everybody traded on what they had, after all, and if what you had wasn't pretty, well, there was still a friend for you.

—

In class on Wednesday, Fetko seemed distracted. When Shipley raised his hand and asked him to expand upon the socioeconomic conditions of the lady with the pet dog, he did so without protest. Later, when Beatrice went to meet him in his office, he wasn't there. A note on his door said he was ill and that office hours had been canceled. Beatrice hoped Fetko's guilt over what had happened between her and Shipley would not jeopardize their arrangement. She had enough on her plate worrying about China without the added anxiety of having to complete his assignments as well.

At a vending machine she purchased lunch–a chocolate bar and pretzels, neither of which would taste like anything, she already knew. She found a bench on a wide walkway in front of the tall Humanities Building, and looked down into the valley at the poor town she had sold ugly clothes to the previous year. It's better up here, she thought, though she knew she would tumble down the hill soon enough.

Moments later she was joined by Shipley, a fat, sweaty guy with a dumb haircut. People's appearances were of little concern to Beatrice. She bedded the handsome and the homely alike. Along with her taste buds had gone her sense of smell, and she didn't miss it. Sex, she believed, should be more of a democratic process, distributed only when a situation-and not a person-merited it.

He presented her with a card depicting Monet's Water Lilies and containing a message that read, Sorry I raped you-Shipley.

"It's not funny, you know," she said, thrusting the card back at him.

He took it. "I know."

"Then what the hell is that?" she said, motioning toward the card. He was picking at it with his wet fingers.

"My parents think I should try to make it up to you."

"Are you retarded or something?"

He laughed, relieved. "You have a great personality."

"You are retarded," she said.

"What are you, some kind of Jesus freak?"

"I'm an atheist."

"Then start talking like one," she said. "Try to remember that your life is worthless."

see interview question V, page 34

Shipley lived with his parents in a suburban house twenty minutes outside of the town in which the university was located. "C'mon in," he said when she rang the doorbell. A black cat with dandruff stood at his feet. "This is Marigold," he said by way of introduction.

"Hi," she said to the cat.

It was the kind of house that suggested two parents: one to earn the money and one to decorate it. Things matched. Upholstery, wood work – photos were displayed. Opened junk mail was nowhere to be found. She suspected the bathrooms would contain certain guest soaps and towels and would be disappointing to clean, as dirt would never be allowed to accumulate. It was a house that reeked of schedules and chore lists. A place where people willingly snacked on carrots. It was the type of house she had trained herself to hate both because she wanted it and because she could safely say it would never be hers.

"Can I take your coat?" Shipley said. He was fidgeting, playing with the waistband of his bright yellow sweatshirt. It didn't extend far enough to completely cover his stomach. This was the duty of the grey t-shirt beneath it. His hair reminded her of a combover without the bald spot and she thought about suggesting to him that he looked about thirty-eight but then fell asleep inside herself at the thought of all the energy it would take. She liked his jeans, she decided.

She tugged her coat around her. "No, thanks," she said. "I might want to to leave early."

"Oh," he said. "We better hurry up then."

He led her through a formal sitting room , through a dining room with a place set for her, and into the kitchen where his parents were cooking together. "Hi!" his mother said as if they were long lost friends. "Beatrice!" his father said. They both wore aprons and were dipping spoons into various pots on the stove, tasting, then sipping, as if there were no question of germs.

His mother set the spoon down and wiped her hands on her apron before extending one to Beatrice. She was a slow moving woman with dry skin and wispy, short hair. Her cheeks were bright pink and it was clear from the complete lack of make-up on her face that this was natural. "So good to meet you, Bea," she said. "Ship has told us so much about you."

"All good!" his father reassured her, even though she didn't care (either way).

"Hi," Beatrice said, feeling several responses behind.

"My parents are very warm, generous people," Shipley said. "I think you'll find that you'll like them.

Beatrice glared at him for putting her in the position of saying, "Yes, I'm sure I will."

"I'm in college," he offered.

"You have some sort of emotional retardation," she surmised, "some sort of freakishness in that way."

He shrugged. Suddenly, a strange concern that she had hurt his feelings came and went. "Well," she said, "I guess I'll take the card back."

He handed it to her, then sat down on the bench. Her nylon book bag lay between them, and she made no attempt to move it. "You're my first," he said.

"Is that right?" she said. She had been many, many firsts.

"That's why you're kind of special to me."

"Uh-huh." She was alternating: a bite of chocolate, a bite of pretzel. Sweet, salt, sweet, salt. It tasted like a little something.

"I'd like you to meet my parents," he said hopefully.

"You're a nice kid," she said. "I don't really like to meet people's parents."

"My mother feeds expired birth control pills to our plants," he said, "to fertilize them."

"Stop talking about that," she snapped.

"Sorry," he said.

They spent the rest of the afternoon like that: together, but not too close.

—

Fetko seemed back to his normal self on Friday. He refused to acknowledge Shipley's request for an accounting of Babel's whereabouts on the eve of the revolution, and was in his office after class. But when Beatrice asked him softly what she would find if she unzipped his pants, he stared back at her blankly. "Beatrice," he said, rubbing his eyes, "I've made a mistake here. We can talk as much as you want-anytime you want-but not about the stuff we used to talk about. And you need to start doing better on your quizzes."

She left his office, stunned. She went home and masturbated, then fell asleep. A call from Shipley woke her at around eleven that night. "What do you want?" she demanded.

At dinner Shipley announced that he was in love with Beatrice.

"You can't say that!" Beatrice protested, her mouth full of sweet potatoes.

"Sorry," Shipley said quickly.

"You've made Beatrice uncomfortable," Mr. Bones said matter of factly. "Those are things you should discuss in private."

"Whoops," Shipley said.

Mrs. Bones said, "I just put up that border last weekend. Whaddya think?"

Beatrice looked up at the parade of country geese running along the top of the walls.

"Huh," Beatrice said.

"Bea may not be a fan of country décor," Mrs. Bones said.

"You're probably more modern," Gretchen agreed.

"Hey, don't forget about the birth control, Mom," Shipley said.

Beatrice dropped her fork and stood up. "Jesus!"

"Sorry," Shipley said.

"Take a walk, Ship,' Mrs. Bones said.

"No," Beatrice said. "I'm leaving."

"No," Shipley said. "Please. Stay here with my parents. I'll take a walk. Really."

After he left, Mr. Bones said, "He's a little nervous." He laughed. "We're all a little nervous."

"It isn't often we get to meet Shipley's friends," Gretchen added. "That's all.

Beatrice sat back down. She finished her meal and answered all Mr. and Mrs. Bones questions about her family, her studies, her apartment in the center of town.

Nobody mentioned Shipley when the time for dessert came around. By the time he came back, Beatrice had taken her coat and shoes off and they were halfway through Wheel of Fortune.

"Wanna go to my room?" Shipley asked her and when she looked to his parents they called out, "Better late than never," and "Better safe than sorry," at the TV.

His room was very clean. Sterile.

"Where did you go?" she asked him, lingering in the doorway. He sat at the edge of his bed, trying to find a radio station that would come in clearly.

"I took Marigold for a walk."

"The cat walks with you?"

"On a leash."

"Cats hate leashes."

"He doesn't mind. I also give him baths."

"You're an idiot," Beatrice said. "Your parents are nice but you're an idiot."

He didn't say anything.

"I'm hoping we're going to make love again sometime soon. When you're awake."

"Forget it." She sat up in bed and noticed how perfectly her square, latticed windows framed an amoebic moon.

"What's the matter?" he asked.

"My boyfriend dumped me."

"You have a boyfriend?"

"Had."

"Wow." He paused for a moment before saying, "Well that's great! Now I have a better chance!"

She laughed for the first time since the explanation of the uncircumcised penis. "I guess you do."

"Really?" he asked, excited.

She woke up a little more. "No."

She went on to tell him about China, as a sort of review for a test she had the next day. He listened intently, and she was surprised at a man more than satisfied by this kind of talk.

—

She failed the test, having spent too much time studying the health of the Chinese--acupuncture and such--as opposed to agriculture and commerce. She wasn't doing much better in Russian literature, where she had begun sitting next to Shipley and passing him questions intended to drive the professor mad. Upon receipt of these, Shipley would instantly raise his hand and ask, "Is Lolita a memoir?" or, "Have you ever been to the Russian circus?" Though Fetko eventually stopped calling on him, Shipley continued to wave his arm around maniacally, complaining frequently of numbness in his fingers. It was during this period that Beatrice first knew herself to giggle.

She could've scared Fetko, she knew--could've threatened to turn him in if he didn't keep her grades up. But the thought of this reminded her too much of that first night with Shipley: how, because she had set out to harm him, the whole thing was really all her fault. In reporting either man she would only incriminate herself-reveal that she was a fraud who would do anything to keep her good grades and student loans. There was

"Cats don't like baths either."

He shrugged. "Are you leaving now?"

"Sorry," she said.

"We could make love."

"Forget it," she said.

"We could kiss."

She didn't see the harm in it and sat down beside him. When he kissed her, he refused to pucker. He instead ran his lips against hers, irritating her.

"There is something wrong with you, isn't there?" she said, sitting up.

"Isn't there something wrong with you?" he said.

"Don't change the subject," she said.


He lived with his mother in an apartment downtown. It was newly built to look old as if it had been there all along, soaking up the secrets of the town with its brick. Beatrice like the idea of instant history — of instant anything—and had an idea that the evening would go well. She found it quaint that she had to pay a parking meter to visit Shipley and planned to ask him for the three quarters back. If necessary, she could tell him she was going out to add more money and never come back.

The place was a terrible disappointment inside. If she hadn't known Shipley's mother was a doctor, she would've guessed it from the woman's living room, a sea of mauve upholstery, glass table tops, portraits of flowers that had never seen a paintbrush. "This room is hurting my eyes," she told Shipley. "Is there another one?"

He took her to the kitchen which was decorated by an abundance of butcher block and a red tiled floor. "Where's your mother?" Beatrice said, seating herself at a small wood table.

"She's not home yet," Shipley said.

"When's she coming home?"

"Soon. She's on rounds."

"I thought you said she wanted to meet me? Where's the birth control?"

"I could make you dinner."

"What kind?"


His mother was a Doctor of Psychology and she didn't have any birth control pills. She did have a colleague in gynecology who gave her expired packets to feed to her plants and it was these Shipley had to offer Beatrice.

At dinner she expressed confusion over the fact that Shipley had never mentioned Beatrice before, except she didn't call him Shipley. She called him Mike. She said, Mike has never kept a girlfriend a secret from me until now.

"I'm not his girlfriend," Beatrice clarified.

"Well maybe that's it," she said.

no point. Her only recourse now was to brace herself, China and Russia having allied themselves against her.

—

Shipley had an old VW van he drove Beatrice around in after class. He bought her lunch with a credit card belonging to a Shipley Sr., and wrote stories in which the two of them met Chekhov and took him to the doctor. He let Beatrice stick a fine sewing needle in his face and insisted it made him feel better all around. Knowing her financial situation, he cut her envelopes of coupons, brought her bags of pharmaceutical samples from his mother's office. They lay side by side on the grassy campus hills, drinking children's cough syrup and chewing Flintstones vitamins until the sun set over the Fine Arts Building and they fell asleep, waking up with bugs and grass in their hair. The word idyllic sprang to Beatrice's mind more than once, but she ignored it, thinking it was probably just anxiety. For when she wasn't with Shipley, she was irritable, unsettled. She had lost track of some of her unhappiness and could not seem to relocate it, not even in the bedrooms of the boys on the second floor-though she had looked.

"Do you remember anything about my penis?" Shipley asked her on the hillside one evening. The pollen count had been high that day, and they were passing a bottle of nasal spray back and forth.

"Not really," Beatrice said.

"Wow," he said.

"Yup," she said. "Imagine that."

"Hey, why did your boyfriend dump you?"

"Why?"

Shipley nodded.

"He was jealous of you," Beatrice said.

"He knows me?"

"He's been watching us," she confirmed.

This silenced Shipley for some time. It was a Sunday during finals, and the campus was deserted. "Would you like to see my penis?" he asked.

She looked over at his crotch. "Is it anything special?"

Even though he was a liar, Beatrice agreed to drive him around in the car after dinner and continued to call him Shipley. She found the turn of events novel and had even taken a packet of the expired birth control pills along at his urging, buying his explanation that milk is still good 6 beyond the sell-by date.

"Do you remember anything about my penis?" he asked her. They were parked on the university campus, at its highest point, in a dorm parking lot.

"Not really," she said.

"Wow," he said.

"Yup," she said. "Imagine that."

He laughed. "Wow," he said again. "Hey, why did your boyfriend dump you?"

"Why?" she said.

He nodded.

"He was jealous of you," she said.

"He knows me?"

"He's been watching us," she confirmed.

This silenced Shipley for some time. "Are you going to take those birth control pills?"

"I might."

"Would you like to see my penis?"

She looked over at his crotch. "Is it anything special?" she asked.

"I think so," he said.

"Actually, I'd like to see your driver's license," she said.

He reached in his wallet and handed it to her. It was a picture of him with a much thinner face, a handsome face. His name was indeed Mike and he was twenty-five and not eighteen. She looked at him personally and saw that this was true.

"I used to look better," he said.

"What happened?" she asked.

"There may be something wrong with me," he acknowledged, "but I'm not taking any drugs."

She handed him back his license. He unbuckled his belt and leaned toward her.

He shrugged. She handed him back the license. She thought about asking him why he lied, but it seemed pointless.

She failed out of school and went back to working at the cheap clothing store. The women who worked there were glad to have her back and spent their days recounting childbirth experiences, the pride they took in their husbands and boyfriends, endless stories about the cuteness of pets.

His mother gave her four packets of pills.

She was very much in the middle of

"I think so," he said.

She nodded. He took it out. "Okay," she said. "I saw it."

"It doesn't ring a bell?"

"No." She passed him the nasal spray.

He inhaled deeply, pinching the side of his empty nostril. "If I left it out," he said, sniffling, "would you do anything with it?"

"Probably not."

"Because I raped you?"

"Probably."

He put it away. "My mother thinks you should go for counseling," he said as he zipped up his fly.

"Why?"

"She says I raped you and you need to face that reality."

"I already did," she said.

"You're supposed to get mad, though."

"I'm busy," she said. "Doesn't your mother know anger is unproductive?"

"Is there anything that would make you want to make love with me again?"

"Yes," she said.

"What is it?" he asked eagerly, but she said she didn't know.

—

She failed out of school and lost her student loans. They hired her back at the cheap clothing store, where she felt oddly invigorated by her co-workers' discussions of impostor perfumes and patio furniture. Shipley picked her up in the evenings in his VW van and drove her to the college, where they continued to lie on the grass and take medication. He told her if they got married people would give them money and small appliances. "I'm tired of trading," she said, and she fell asleep.

And yet she couldn't bring herself to sleep with Shipley. It had little to do with his appearance, though people told her he smelled. The problem lay in his ability to please her. The unfamiliarity of this was stressful, even repulsive at times. She was twenty-two and about to become settled in her ways. All her life she had been desperate to become an old dog, to get to the point where no one would consider that she might be able to change. She was working toward something definite now – a kind of certainty. He might change her, but he would never ever get her. She would see to that. He had made everything in her life unrecognizable and this was not to be forgiven.

"It's because I raped you, isn't it?"
"Probably," she said.
"You can never forgive me."
"I forgive you."
"I just couldn't stop myself. I knew it was wrong, but I couldn't stop."
"Do you know that Fetko doesn't like you?" Beatrice said.
"Sure," he said.
"Maybe he drove you to rape me."
"I don't think so," Shipley said.
"I guess not," she said.
"Does Fetko like you?" he said.
She thought for a minute. "Yes, I think so."
"Because you're pretty."
"Yes."
"Well," he said. " I wish it hadn't happened."
"Well it did," she said.
"You can never forgive me."

She failed out of school and went back to work at the cheap clothing story. She felt oddly invigorated by her co-workers' talk of imposter perfumes and patio furniture. Shipley picked her up in the evenings in his VW van and drove her to the college where they continued to lay on the grass and take medicine. He told her if they got married people would give them money and small appliances. "You could meet my parents, even," he said, and she told him he couldn't possibly make it sound less enticing. "Could I meet your parents?"

Then one day, Fetko came into the store with his wife. It was a weekday, so only she and one other woman were working and the other woman was at lunch. Fetko seemed startled to see her and immediately told his wife he didn't think she would find anything she liked here but she told him to sit down in the chair by the dressing room and wait. "What would you know" she said, and so Fetko shuffled by the cash register where Beatrice stood and flopped down in the chair.

Beatrice watched him for a moment and thought all professors dressed as if it were 1974. She thought how amazing it was that young women of the 90s got crushes on them, as if being smarter and older transcended fashion. She had never had a crush on Fetko—he'd had

On a Tuesday in May, Fetko came into the clothing store with his wife. Summer was slow in retail, and so it was just Beatrice, her manager having stepped out for lunch. Fetko seemed startled to see her and immediately told his wife he didn't think she would find anything she liked here, but she told him to sit down in the chair by the dressing room and wait. "What do you know anyway?" she said, and so Fetko shuffled past Beatrice at the cash register, his eyes glued to the floor.

Beatrice watched him for a moment, thinking about how most male professors his age—maybe fifty—still dressed as if it were 1974. She thought how amazing it was that young, stylish women of the nineties managed to get crushes on them anyway, as if age and intelligence transcended fashion. She had never had a crush on Fetko, and suddenly regretted this. He was a depressed, inappropriate, badly dressed man, and all she had ever noticed was his grade book, his red pencil.

Beatrice approached his chair now, which was puce where it wasn't threadbare. "Can I offer you a magazine or something to drink, sir?" she asked. She had no magazine or drinks. It was a cheap store. But she was stirred by his grief and did not want it to end.

"No thanks," he said. Then he added, "Miss."

Beatrice nodded. "I'll just help your wife then," she said, and walked off.

Mrs. Fetko was stout and seemed drawn to a group of coordinating, boxy separates done up in feminine, floral prints. "May I say you have lovely skin, ma'am," Beatrice began, which was the truth. Mrs. Fetko laughed and reached into her purse for a business card. "Here's my secret, hon," she said, handing it to Beatrice. Full Body Massage by Jules, it read. "You can keep it," she added. "Now, what do you think about this?" She held up a pink-and-gray blouse and a matching gray skirt.

"Is there a special occasion?" Beatrice asked.

"My husband works up at the college and he was just awarded an endowed chair. Very impressive. So I need something to wear to the ceremony. How about this?" She had laid the pink group over her arm and was now into the teals.

Beatrice shrugged. "They're just the same exact things in different colors."

Mrs. Fetko laughed. "Tell it like it is! I love it. Here. Start a dressing room for me, babe."

Beatrice took the clothes from her and headed toward the back of the store, where Fetko was furiously examining a dry-cleaning receipt

one on her—but now, in his suffering, she began to sense his appeal.

"Can I offer you a magazine or something to drink, sir?" she said. She had no magazine or drinks. It was a cheap store. But something about his unhappiness was stirring her, and she wanted to feel this more.

"No thanks," he said. Then he added, "Miss."

Beatrice nodded. "I'll just help your wife then."

Mrs. Fetko was stout and seemed drawn to a coordinating group of separates that compensated for their boxy cut with feminine floral prints. Sometimes, when business was slow, Beatrice's co-workers dressed her up in these clothes and gave themselves a laugh. They said the funniest part was how unhappy Beatrice always looked while wearing, how she never laughed at herself, not even when she looked in the mirror. "Why should I?" she would tell them.

"Can I help you, ma'am?" Beatrice said.

"Yes, dear," she said. "My husband teaches up at the college and he's been given an endowed chair. They'll be having a ceremony and I need to look my best. How about this?" She pulled a grey jacket and skirt off the rack and a coordinating pink and grey blouse.

"That's nice," Beatrice said.

"Put it in the dressing room for me, will you dear?"

"Sure," Beatrice said.

"I'll just pick a few more things."

"Ok," Beatrice said.

She headed for the back of the store. Fetko was intently reading a piece of paper from his wallet which looked to be a dry cleaning receipt.

After she'd started a room for Mrs. Fetko, Beatrice told him, "Congratulations on your award."

He looked up from his receipt. "Thank you."

"Do you remember me?" she said.

"Of course," he said. "Please."

'Just wondering," she said.

Mrs. Fetko tried on several outfits, none of which looked any better or worse than the last. When she asked Fetko which one he liked best, he said he didn't care. She pressed him and he said, "The pink." Mrs. Fetko went back to try it on again.

"Look," Fetko whispered when his wife was gone. "I'm sorry. Ok?"

Beatrice shrugged.

"No one was forcing you to do anything," he said.

"I know."

He took out a handkerchief and wiped his brow. "You should've turned that kid into the police."

"Could one of you give me a hand back here?" Mrs. Fetko called.

"You go," Fetko said. "I can't help her."

Beatrice pulled the curtain aside to find Mrs. Fetko half undressed, a price tag from the blouse caught in the chain of her necklace. "I can't seem to free myself," she said.

from his wallet. She put Mrs. Fetko's clothes in a cubicle and said, "Congratulations," when she came back out.

He looked up from his receipt blankly.

"On your award," Beatrice added.

"Thank you," he whispered.

"Do you remember me?" she asked.

"Of course I do," he hissed. "Please!"

"Just wondering," she said.

Mrs. Fetko tried on several outfits, none of which was any better or worse than the others. When she asked Fetko which one he liked best, he said he didn't know. She pressed him and he said, "The pink, okay?"

"Don't be such an ass, Fetko," she said, rolling her eyes at Beatrice before returning to the dressing room.

"What are you looking at?" Fetko asked Beatrice after his wife had gone.

"Nothing," she said.

He glanced at the dressing rooms, then back at Beatrice. "Say something good to me," he whispered, laying a hand across his groin. "Quick."

She said something. He closed his eyes and smiled a little, the way he used to do. "Say something else," he said, and she did.

In return he offered her nothing. There were no more grades left, no student loans. Furthermore, he had clearly come to understand that she wouldn't retaliate. She had never once complained about the D he had given her, never hinted she even knew of the trouble she could cause him. And now here he was, looking to gratify himself at her expense. Asking for a freebie. She had complied not out of fear or hopefulness, but rather gratitude, for at last she felt herself to be depleted, empty, and in need.

—

In the van on the way home she told Shipley she loved him. "Will we make love?" he asked hopefully.

"Probably not," she said. "It's not that kind of love."

Beatrice saw that the string and the chain were entwined in such a way that it seemed unbelievable they could have gotten that way on their own. She picked at it with her fingernails for several minutes while Mrs. Fetko waited patiently under the blouse, breathing lightly.

"How's it coming?" she asked periodically, and Beatrice said she was getting there. What was taking so long was that she was Mrs. Fetko and Beatrice couldn't keep her eyes from passing over the woman's fleshy back, the wisps of hair on her neck. It was from this that she had once enticed him. A patient woman had moved out of the seventies who for better of worse had grown old and now wore the styles of the day.

"What's going on back there?" Fetko called.

And they called back, "Nothing" for Mrs. Fetko was now free and thankful to Beatrice.

Shipley had given up on her.

8

"My mother thinks you should go for counseling."

"Why?"

"She says I raped you and you need to face that reality."

"I already did."

"You're supposed to get mad, though."

"I'm busy," she said. "Doesn't your mother know anger is unproductive?"

"Is there anything that would make you want to make love with me again?"

"Yes," she said.

"What is it?" he said eagerly, but she said she didn't know. Together they tried to figure out what it might be. Shipley wore deodorant and stopped talking about the rape and his penis so much.

9

"Say something to me now," Fetko said.

She did.

"Say another thing."

She did.

In return, he offered her nothing. There were no more grades left, no more student loans. He had made his request knowing she wouldn't retaliate. He was looking to make himself happy at her expense and for a brief moment she considered that this might be love.

10

10In the van on the way home, she told him she loved him.

"Will we make love?" he asked hopefully.

"Probably not," she said. "It's not that kind of love."

"Oh," he said. "Could you at least stop sleeping with everybody else?"

"Maybe," she said.

"How about meeting my parents?"

"We'll see," she said.

"Oh," he said. "Well, maybe you could stop making love with everybody else."

"I'll think about it," she said.

"Really?" he asked.

"Sure."

They drove through town without saying much more. The old van heaved and lurched while Shipley coaxed it on for one more mile, up one more city hill. Beatrice noticed a woman at a bus stop wearing a dress from her store, and pointed this out to Shipley, who said she didn't look half bad from a distance. "My mother likes your store," he said. "She said she may come in this weekend."

Beatrice considered protesting but then remembered that the shop was a public place. "What does your mother look like?" she asked instead.

Shipley thought for a minute before saying, "My father," which was of no help whatever.

Later, on the way to the college, Beatrice felt herself wanting more to eat than just medicine, and mentioned as much to Shipley. They planned an elaborate evening of food and drink, then stopped off for ice cream before dinner. It was very wrong of them, and it tasted very good.

# Interview

What was the impetus for this story? What compelled the original draft?
Where and when were you in your life and writing career?

# Alicia Erian:

I had a friend who had once confessed to me that his first sexual experience had been with a girl who had agreed to sleep with him, then passed out. He was deeply ashamed that he'd gone ahead without her. So much so that he revealed to her what he'd done the next morning, and pressured her to take a Morning After Pill. I believe this was at the suggestion of his mother, who was a pediatrician. I might've made the suggestion part up, but my friend at least knew of The Pill from his mother, who was indeed a pediatrician.

I found this story deeply compelling. Anything with great shame attached to it is something I want to write about. Shame, for me, provokes the best work. I also, as I'm sure most women do, have a huge fear of being raped. Maybe I was trying to cut my anxieties a little with the dark humor of the story, I don't know. More than that, though, I think I found my friend's story very interesting because it seemed to me that he had, in fact, technically raped this girl, and yet she didn't give a shit. She just wanted him to leave her alone so that she could forget the whole thing. I do think she ended up taking The Pill in real life, though. Also, my friend is such a nice person. I found it very moving that this exceedingly kind man had made this one bad decision that ended up haunting him for years. It was so against his nature. But sex often creates a sort of alternate headspace in people, a place where they might be willing to suspend everything that they know and believe about themselves and for a time, become someone different.

There were two other elements to the story: the first was the character of Shipley. Instead of basing him on my friend, I based him on a guy I'd known in college who'd had a huge crush on me and was the funniest person I'd ever met. But something was off with him. I wasn't sure what. Years later, I would realize it was likely Asperger's. Anyway, I'd always wished that I could've been his girlfriend because I loved his parents and he made me laugh so incredibly hard. Plus, he loved me so much. It would've been perfect. But I didn't feel attracted to him.

And Fetko is based on the father of another friend. He was a professor and sort of randy and I always thought he was kind of a funny guy. I could imagine falling for him as a student.

Beatrice is the much cooler and calculating aspect of my overall chaotic self. She's also depressed, and very pragmatic. I like her because she never seems particularly worried about not having high expectations for herself.

EDITORS:

It seems to me that *not* writing is one of the most difficult aspects of being
a writer. Certainly in many writers' careers there have been creatively
fallow eras, for any number of reasons. Could you discuss the challenges
as well as the benefits of not writing and then what compelled you to take
it up again?

# Alicia Erian:

I believe this story was the second one I wrote for my first collection of stories. The first story was "Bikini." I would say that "Superpowers" was my first stab at a dirty story, though I had not at all anticipated at the time that it would end up as such. At that point in my life, however, I was married to a man whom I loved deeply, but with whom I did not have a romantic relationship. We had so much else that we felt was meaningful between us at the time, however, that we felt we could deal with the unsatisfying sex life. What I realized many years later, however, was that the lack of intimacy in my marriage started to become something I chased down in my fiction. Put more crudely, I was horny all the time and always thinking about sex, which meant that I also ended up writing about it. When I was done with this story, I both loved it and felt ashamed of it. I told myself, "Okay, you had your fun. Now shape up and write something decent!" Except I never did, for many years. Only when I met my current partner and got the sex life I wanted did I lose interest in sexually-themed fiction. But then I stopped writing altogether for completely different reasons that I discuss in my upcoming memoir.

I was miserable at all times when I wasn't writing. And really, I suppose it's not true that I wasn't writing. I was working on screenplays and TV pilots, one of which Alan Ball very kindly worked with me on and eventually took to HBO (they said no). But I wasn't writing books. And a lot of my feelings of self-worth derive from the act of writing books. Not to mention the fact that it's where I get most of my catharsis. So when I wasn't writing books, I felt myself to be, frankly, sort of worthless. This was pretty challenging, especially since I was a new mother twice over during this period, and needed to stay mentally afloat for my kids. I would attribute my issues to post-partum depression except that I had them pre-partum, too. The problem was that I was in an abusive relationship and couldn't seem to get out. The space in my head was at all times consumed with this relationship, as opposed to with what it should've been consumed with, which was my own life and mental health.

There are three reasons why I started writing again: one, my second child miraculously decided that he didn't want to nurse after eight months, so I could get back on my beloved Adderall, which I require to write, given my raging ADD. Two, I was under contract with Crown to deliver two books, neither of which had actually been written. They were getting, understandably, pretty mad. And three, I was in such incredible distress over the relationship I was in that I knew if I didn't write about it, I'd lose my mind. This book really ended up saving my life. I found my voice again, I found my self-worth, and was finally able to start behaving with some self-respect. The writer Nina de Gramont, also one of my dearest friends, told me when my marriage was breaking up during the time when I wrote *Towelhead*, "Jasira will save you." She was right. I was in

In your first draft, the dialogue between Beatrice and Shipley stands out III as some of the sharpest prose, and entire sections show up, unchanged, in the final draft. It really seems like their interactions are what initially structured the story. Can you talk a bit about how you found the structure of this story? Did you key in on the dialogue and build the story around that, or was it plot that pulled you through, or a more organic combination of parts?

I love your first draft because it's big and wandering and messy; you IV jump in and out of scenes, various backstories, different subplots. It almost seems like you're trying them on for size, writing in different directions until you hit a dead end, and then starting again. Is this a usual sort of drafting process for you? Does your creative process look similar from story to story?

# Alicia Erian:

the deepest depression, and sitting down to write about this girl and her own miseries every day didn't help on the surface, but it created this book that ended up improving my life in many ways. This memoir has already done the same, and it hasn't even been published yet. When I feel bad about the last six and a half years of my life, I always remind myself that this book wouldn't have come into existence without them, and it is my sincere hope that what I've written will mean something to someone besides me.

I knew I wanted to start the story with the rape/pseudo-rape scene, depending on how one views it. As I said above, the scenario for the story came from an experience a friend of mine had, but then I replaced the character of my friend with another friend from college, and made the woman in bed with him a version of myself. I was looking for some kind of forum in which to discuss my relationship with this man I really wanted to love but couldn't. In reality, we did have terrifically funny conversations. He would let me boss him around endlessly, and I really ran amok at times. He also thought everything that I said was hilarious, no matter how insulting. He never seemed to take anything personally. And he was completely unaware of how odd he was. No, that's not true. He was aware, but he didn't care.

In terms of actual structure, I never plot out a story. The thought of doing that is something I find terrifying. All I ever know at the beginning of the story is how it's going to start. The excitement for me as a writer is watching the whole thing unfold.

Actually, I'm being a little disingenuous. When I start a story, I generally know what most of the elements will be (randy professor, depressed narrator with bad grades, etc.), along with the opening scene. What I should say is that I don't have any plan for how the elements will mash up against one another.

I felt really sorry for you that you had to transcribe that thing. But yes, it's true, I'm a messy drafter sometimes. Not all of the time, but sometimes. In those moments in the draft where I jump out of the story or leave a scene hanging, or run something until I can see it's going nowhere, I'm usually struggling, or even panicked. I'll try a million things, then backtrack to the point where I got frustrated and attempt to refocus, then jump around some more. Those are bad writing days, and I tend to feel horrible at the end of them. Later, though, when I'm making dinner or doing something else not writing-related, I'll think back on some snippet I wrote and decide that there might be something there.

# EDITORS:

Related: why did you ultimately decide not to develop the scenes with     V
Shipley's parents and Beatrice?

So the story starts off with a rape that is not acknowledged as a rape by     VI
Beatrice. This is startling and hilarious and also kind of makes me worry
about Beatrice (but I start to lose this concern as the story progresses).
Were you every worried that you'd be criticized for this move at the
beginning of the story? (Have you even been criticized?)

Let's talk about dark humor since this story is full of it: the alleged rape,     VII
Beatrice's nonchalance toward Fetko's perversions, her ambivalence
at failing out of school. For writers who might be experimenting with
dark humor in their own stories, what advice or anecdotes do you have
for others exploring this mode? What are some favorite pieces of dark
humor, whether in literature or some other art form, that you admire?

# Alicia Erian:

Hmm. I'm not sure if I can remember my rationale. I wrote this story roughly fourteen years ago. My best guess now is that those scenes rendered the story flabby. Or else my ex-husband, who edited my first two books, told me to do it and I did. He was a spectacular editor. The official editors for both of my books had almost nothing to do when I turned them in, thanks to my ex.

*I was* worried that I'd be criticized, but I haven't been, as far as I recall. Or maybe I have been and don't know about it. I understood that it was a garish opening but I also loved that about it. I loved the real and terrible story that had inspired it, and it seemed reasonable enough to want to tell. I imagined that there were likely many readers who would be able to identify with the idea of a scenario like this, one that isn't quite illegal, but also feels beyond just a mistake. There was intent on the part of Shipley, and yet there is also intent on the part of Beatrice to opt out of ruminating over the circumstances. He is pushing her to play the victim, something that she seems to find vulgar. She'd much rather be the victimizer with both Shipley and Fetko, until it becomes clear that Fetko is really the one in control, manipulating her in the clothing store. Only here does Beatrice finally acknowledge some feelings of distress, which in turn set her free a little. She still can't love Shipley, but she can better understand his love for her, and perhaps be a little nicer to him, a little less disgusted.

What I will say about the opening scene is that I worry every time I read the story to an audience that I am causing distress to someone who is listening, since statistically, there is likely someone in the audience who has been raped. The problem for me as a writer is that it's one of my shorter stories, which makes it good for readings, and the dialogue really moves things along, so that the audience doesn't get too bored. So part of me will think, No, I shouldn't read this, but then it often ends up being the best choice.

I love the narrator in Carver's "Cathedral," who is so incredibly politically incorrect and insensitive and rude, while at the same time pretending that he's not. He is freaking hilarious. Also, Denis Johnson's "Emergency" is one of the funniest stories ever. It's all situational. People doing things they're not supposed to do in certain settings, like taking drugs in an ER or acting like they're a doctor when they're really a doped-up orderly. And I remember laughing a lot when I read *Diary of a Nobody* in college, as well as *A Confederacy of Dunces*. I don't watch a lot of fictional TV, but *The Office* has always had some pretty good dark humor, I think, as well as early seasons of *It's Always Sunny in Philadelphia*. I can't comment on later seasons because I stopped watching for some reason.

EDITORS:

I found Beatrice's psychology in this story incredibly compelling. She    VIII
isn't victimized by her choices. There's not a deep psychic wound after
her experience with Shipley or with Fetko. She is profoundly (and oddly)
capable despite her flaws. Your portrayal of a young woman is refreshing
and surprising and dare I say emancipating. Your entire collection, in
fact, has an array of women who I don't see often in short stories. Can
you talk about your approach to writing women characters and telling
their stories?

# Alicia Erian:

It's really hard to talk about how to be funny in one's writing, I've found. Part of the issue for me was that I never set out to be funny. But when my ex-husband started editing for me, he would laugh and laugh. At first I was offended. I would say, "What are you doing? Why are you laughing at that? That's not supposed to be funny!" And he'd say, "Um, but it is." That was an interesting experience. Because then I had to sort of reframe how I saw what I was doing. Things that seemed serious to me were coming off very differently to others.

Someone once told me in a grad school workshop that they were confused about my characters, and wondered if these were in fact retarded adults. This reader was 100% serious. Not kidding at all. I wasn't really sure what to do with this. Part of me thought it was interesting, and even complimentary somehow, but another part of me thought, But I'm writing from my own perspective here. And I am not a retarded adult. At the same time, I often felt—and still feel—myself to know and understand next to nothing about anything, even as I also obviously know at least a few things. I guess my point is, a lot of humor comes from voice. For me, a voice that has often seemed natural to fall into is that of the character who is imposing his or her singular view on everything and everyone around her, so that nothing outside of his/her world seems to make any sense. This is something that I do find funny—the mess that ensues when we assume that we are somehow more universal than we really are.

So that's humor derived from character. Another brand of humor is one derived from situations. The best thing you can do for yourself as a writer, in my opinion, is pick a scenario that is odd and peculiar enough, while also being accessible in its way, so that every scene that follows will also somehow have to be slightly askew. There's never any need for pointed humor when you force your characters into situations that absolutely shouldn't exist but are believable to the reader nevertheless.

These women are all very much based on some aspect of me and/or my life, combined with others in my life, or stories I've heard from people I know. "Bikini" is about a fight my mother and father had while sailing before they got married. I was terrified of my father growing up, and always loved how unafraid my mother was of him. "On the Occasion of My Ruination" is basically the story of how I lost my virginity. Probably the least fictionalized piece in the book. "When Animals Attack" is about a brother and sister (based on my brother and me) who take out their rage toward their mother on a poor kid who means them no harm.

As I write down these brief synopses, it occurs to me that so many of these women are related to my mother. She was always a very difficult person for me, but I also admired and loved her. She was really funny and rude and had a lot of balls. She also raised my brother and me on

EDITORS:

Do you have any revision techniques, tricks or tips that you could share   |X ————
with our readers?

# Alicia Erian:

her own, though my grandparents helped a lot (they appear in "Still Life With Plaster," probably my favorite story in the book, not least because I did find someone with a motorcycle license to tussle with—again, see next year's memoir). She was a very acidic person, often impossible to be around. But she was also a great feminist, and never anyone who taught me to think in terms of limits. She was a smart woman, a librarian, and she thought it was the greatest thing in the world that I wanted to be a writer, even when I started writing negatively about her. She let my brother and me run amok a lot of the time because she was too depressed to take care of us, so we had more freedom than most kids in many ways. She told me all her personal problems, which she should never have done, but she also listened to my suggestions and acted like they were really smart. We led a very boundary-less life with her, which screwed me up hugely, but also allowed me to see the world in ways I likely never would have otherwise. If you were having a coughing fit around my mother, she would never ask you sympathetically if you were all right. She would gripe in an irritated voice, "Stop that!" This is so wrong and it wasn't fun to grow up with. But it's also very funny. And since I loved her, I was able to look at other people who did wrong things in the world and also find them lovable. This was bad for my personal life, but good for my writing life.

For me, if I have to make more than about three revision passes at a piece of work, it probably sucks. In other words, revise well, but don't revise endlessly. Know when to quit. And stories don't have to be perfect. Just good enough. A good enough good story is a thing of beauty. Don't knock it. Also, force yourself to take breaks. The answer usually comes on a break. And you have to read out loud several times as you go. That's really the test for me. It has to sound good out loud. That's also where I can hear the boring, overwritten parts, of which there are generally many! And figure out some really smart friends who can edit you reliably. You need these people.

# Donald Dunbar

## Excerpt from
## *Eyelid Lick*

DRAFT  FINAL

# DRAFT

Dear Clive Owen,

Thankfully this will be able to reach you, Clive Owen.

Here are the lists of question that I am supposed to incorporate in my research paper. Any information is hopeful if anyone can email me back to let me know that I am not an emailing robot that would really help me a lot.

- ☐ I smashed my hand with the gauze on it into the table because it was hurting and then the blood would be dripping down my arm when it would reopen and I'd run at the workers and attack them?
- ☐ Why is the economy so fucking shitty goddamn it?
- ☐ You're not hungry at all? (No I just ate)
- ☐ The bottled blood and the synthetic blood, that would be my drink of choice?
- ☐ My body cracks when it needs to and so does mine?
- ☐ No?
- ☐ You're calling to say hi?
- ☐ Is that what that word means l-u-c-r-e?

Your responsibilities may delay your responses to these questions, I would like to let you know that should I receive good responses from you I appreciated it.

Sincerely yours,
Donald Dunbar

# Final

Dear God,

In regards to your honesty, I think the poorest of the poor deserve it the most,
and then the second-poorest.
God, they will listen.
Show you their rare affection.
Like adding thickener to your tears.
In regards to your honesty, toughing out the economy.

You see, it's a shame and the future is all a goddamn mess, it is awful I'm here to say! I see one way and then I see another, and there comes this point that all you're looking at is looked at through tears.

They fall silently through flowering trees in a late spring snow.

God, my darling girl cat lost today, and though it fought long battles with diseases it was devastating to both of us. She didn't die alone. I was here the entire time.

We were so connected,

Dear Clive Owen,

In my issues Democrats have run inner cities, public schools, universities, unions, manufacturing, black churches, for decades, all bamboozled, Upset that we are NOT openly attacking these Democrats! I mean hardcore Hollywood Democrats, after they easily accuse me of racism when I say your Democrats have run inner cities for 40 years, hows that been going? I'm upset that you are not blatant against the Democrats and regulations, openly attacking like open health care markets, like abortions and housing loans, like open ERs killing hospital's budget. Democrats create regulations to ruin it then claim more regulations to solve it,

I know, but its got to be more!

SOLVE: bring more direct accusations of Democrat failures like inner cities, universities, more exposure of school textbooks, of force fed Hollywood Democrat issues to their fullest. If they want MY issues or if they want condoms in schools, if they want inner cities, public schools, manufacturing, then get a law allowing to have kids have sex at home! If they want racism, ruin it and accuse me! I think the future is going to be awful! Like universities, unions, black churches, it has my hope right out of me.

What do you think: MORE attacks against Democrats, or allowing to have kids have sex at school, open ERs and hospitals!

Thank you Clive Owen,
Donald Dunbar

Rather than try harder to reach you, I have opted into a new plan for communication:

Really Speaking Your Heart.

The thing is, in reaching you such, if your heart doesn't recognize the product of mine, well who's to know? For instance, if I were to put it to song:

Dear Clive Owen,

In regards to your charity, well what do you know!
In regards to your charity, you have given so much already, Clive Owen, please can you give more??
In regards to your charity. I think the poorest of the poor deserve it the most, and then the second-poorest.
Clive Owen, we will do tricks for you.
Show you our rare affection.
In regards to your charity, there are so many things to care about and you do that so well.
Clive Owen, your charity is solidarity!
In regards to your charity, our loving hearts shoulder any burden, don't they?
In regards to your charity, toughing out the economy.

You see, it's a shame and the future is all a goddamn mess, it's awful I'm here to say! I see one way and then I see another, and there comes this point that all you're looking at is looked at through tears.

They fall silently through flowering trees in a late spring snow.

I kind of have a feeling adding gluten to your face when you're crying produces special effects.

Clive Owen, my darling girl cat lost today, and though it fought long battles with diseases it was devastating to both of us. She didn't die alone. I was here the entire time.

We were so connected,
Donald Dunbar

but I sang it at so high a frequency only children would hear it, sure I'm being honest but am I being honest to you?

For instance, I really love it when newscasters fuck up!

And when I'm in love with someone and I sometimes feel like that, totally fucking up! "excuse me" and connector words containing nothing of the whole beast I feel because it wouldn't let one part of itself away.

And someone's likely to not understand at first, when they do understand am I then communicating honestly?

Dear Clive Owen,

Clive Owen! I hate you! Hahaha!!

In the year I was born, three things happened: one) I was burned on the leg by hot boiling water two) instead of a love for the theater (in actors playing and walking on stages) I developed a love for movies (NO actors live) and three) I was born. Dear Clive Owen,

Hey, I'm thinking about you,
Donald Dunbar

Or when I'm talking to someone in love yes but hoping to be overheard too, but then I'm into that kind of intimacy.

Dear Clive Owen,

Everything's for sale in the UK, even a name. But in the US where we do not have a strong sense of history and everything's run by big corporations (BIG PHARMA, BIG OIL, BIG FARM CHEMICALS), everything is about Christianity and Muslims. And I wonder, what's the best part about heaven?

How does it (Heaven) compare with death?

Please if you would cut out this part of a letter and return it to me with enough postage for "overseas".

        PRO:

        CON:

If you receive this instead as an email attached, you will please document this. I have a "blog" and you will be able to read more about what I am thinking. For instance, after 9/11 I kind of thought there would be a terrorist attack here. I almost wish it had been. If I was a terrorist I don't think I would do that, as I fear heaven and death! Hahaha!!

Thank you Clive Owen,
Donald Dunbar

x

o

Dear Clive Owen,

You know how it starts, and you know how it ends.

Donald Dunbar

Wait.

[Appendix: Alice Fulton]

She actually put her heart inside of your heart inside of my heart!


"She's kicking, ohh! Oh, she's kicking!"
Alice Fulton is in the freezer! She can't get out! Mally and Lucy put her there, just to see. Now they're pushing against the freezer door, hooting.
"Come on Alice Fulton," yells Mally, "put your fingers in the ice cube tray!"
"Come on Alice Fulton," yells Lucy, "put your feet in the bag of ice for parties!"


She has clay-colored skin that looks like wet clay when she steps out of the shower / and into the bright and terrible room.


All morning and afternoon she draws her fingernails up
and then down
and then up
and then up
and down my heart, hello, this has been exhausting!


And in front of the moon in deep, glorious summer, when three layers of sweat have formed on our skin and dissolved back again, I lean into her, grab her hair at the roots with my right hand, put my left hand over her hand and kiss her!


"Hello? Rawling!" says Lucy, who has now got one foot up on the fridge as she's pulling on the handle to the freezer, "A little fucking help?"
"Come on out Alice Fulton," yells Mally, "we know you're in there!"


And as we kiss, her lips are pulled into mine, and her tongue from between her lips, and from her tongue her heart is pulled into my mouth like a thick, knotty minnow.

Now, the pumping of the heart is inside my body, but it's not specifically for me.

And as my saliva begins to digest it, the heart continues to pump / but like the heart of a forest full of crickets...

Dear Clive Owen,

The following is a supposedly true story:

The father, crying and wailing, begs his son to drink again.
An independent woman is starting her own business.
One bright, beautiful Sunday morning everyone
wakes up and chants "Take another drink!"
Pretty soon she realized she needed a drink and so she began
drinking.

Besides being true,
the story is most likely strange, weird, surprising, or funny.

Before the service starts, the townspeople sit in their pews
and talk about their lives and their families.
Yes, father, yes, mother, I am pregnant and drunk.
Suddenly, in the bar, two men dressed in black coats drink.
Everyone starts screaming
and running for the front entrance
trampling each other.
Swoooop! By now the boy is getting tipsy.
Swoooop! He reaches down, grabs his drink and guzzles the last of it.

I have never understood why the truth of the story, and still it doesn't
make much sense. Is it a secret? Is it important for the meaning of it to
be explainable? I think of curling up into a ball under my blankets and
kissing my knee and pressing lightly on the back of one shoulder. Can I
explain this to you? Why I thought of this story right now!

Thank you Clive Owen, you understand perfectly,
Donald Dunbar

Accordingly, I was granted that which I desired most, and I took it. And when I was asked to explain myself, I no longer had to. The guards had lost any desire to capture me, and the bankers had donated their sperm to the relief effort. Actually, the money was then used to buy me, from you. You now feel an overwhelming, denaturing sense of loss. Thus. A little later, three hundred thousand versions of me swarm into you like drums, and you are pregnant now, with my three hundred thousand children. That which I desired most, the three hundred thousand yous is now acceleratingly three-point-three hundred thousand yous / screaming thirty-three hundred million names for me / through your shorting synapses. Dear God, thou givest and you give, and a little later, well, you get back. Here is a word of power. There is a word retreating. Now, a word reeled back in to the bottom of my stomach and concealed like a pearl. Now, every word is a name / and every name is a note, / U, U, / stacked like cups through your shape and your mind. As in: every part of every cell has inside it the shape for every cell. Honestly, that which I desired most was a more marketable solipsism: your name pasted onto everything, when every word is the same prayer, and all language holy. No, three thousand thous and three thousand yous stacked like glittering identities in the sunshine and melting. Door cleaves open.

Clive Owen,

I think about a world in which the appearance of everything becomes unplugged from all the things. It will look like everyone is walking around buying groceries and folding clothes, but that's only the appearance; the thing is, you won't know where you're going. Unless you've memorized your whole environment, unless everybody had, everyone will be bumping into things and getting into accidents. The only path to survival is sitting perfectly still. As at first the hours pass the shouting will quiet. Then, after a day the last cellphone will die. As years pass it will seem perfectly natural that no one would speak. Decades, hundreds of millions of years not one being will move but it will appear as if they do, the show will surround us all and will have nothing to do with us.

Every so often in the unidentifiable hiss of the world the image of us will appear sitting just as we are sitting, just where we are.

How long, then, before we don't even think anymore to anticipate this?

Thank you Clive Owen,
Donald Dunbar

p.s. When you think about a world and the appearance of it has become detached from the world itself, I feel like you're almost my image wandering around far beyond my perception.

[Appendix: Diagram of Writing Paper and Dying]

Anjie's talking to him about her boyfriend, Cardiff, in a way obviously meant to lead him on, that I'm writing a research paper on? As I research and bibliography, Anjie takes his hand without any warning, puts her hand over his, actually locking himself outside the submarine. His own speargun had ripped a hole in his wetsuit in the battle with the squid, but the keys were gone. And re-research, and re-bibliography. He wants to, in that i-dunno way, though there is almost no information publicly available on my research paper, to touch her shoulder? In my research paper on my research paper, most of my facts are guesses, some documents are stolen, Cardiff is no good, she says, I wish I could be with a nice guy. Now something just like death is in my paper, and I didn't put it there. He says, well, Cardiff is just difference in communications, he says, well, Cardiff is just bad at communicating, Anjie, now death has entered my paper. Because he got back to the submarine with an eighth of a tank of oxygen, he was stupid, being naturally heroic, and it begins pacing the sentences with me, I write a sentence, but it sounds like maybe, and in an across-the-street way, you two aren't, death writes a sentence, fully compatible, too. Anjie draws her hand back, and turns away. Rawling, she says, I'm sorry. He's what I like, you don't understand. He was exploring an underwater trench and drowned, you want to hear how he died?

You don't understand, God,

I understand so little and the world's a mystery I'm here to say! The world is one huge    intimacy—

I forgive you, God,

I forgive with my eyes closed. He walks up, I close my eyes, and forgive. She's already forgiven me though she doesn't know it. Forgive me, I forgive you, after all. I close my eyes and then it's only hearing and then I go deaf. It is then I forgive you.

But inside my forgiveness there's something different too. I close my eyes, she walks up, she plucks my forgiveness from somewhere and it's like there's a seed inside it. Or an egg. She does something else, I forget exactly, but she puts it to her open mouth, closes her eyes—

You find yourself standing in a forest with your eyes closed. The trees here are primarily oak and palm, and > inventory

You have:
| | |
|---|---|
| Head: | Golden-black hair |
| Body: | Golden body paint |
| Right hand: | Palm |
| Left hand: | Rabbit skeleton |
| Feet: | Black loafers (bloody) |

You find yourself standing in a forest with your eyes closed. The trees here are making a low humming noise, and you hear five and then four and then three cascading series of quick clicks and whiffs as insects take off and land in the grass around you. You begin to feel another set of eyelids close over your own...

Democrats have run inner cities, public schools, universities, unions, manufacturing, black churches, for decades, all bamboozled, I mean hardcore Hollywood Democrats, after they easily accuse me of racism when I say your Democrats have run inner cities for 40 years, hows that been going?

[my beautiful friend]

You are not blatant against the Democrats and regulations, openly attacking like open health care markets, like abortions and housing loans, like open ERs killing hospital's budget. Democrats create regulations to ruin it then claim more regulations to solve it,

[come with me]

I know, but its got to be more!

[looking for it]

Bring more direct accusations of Democrat failures like inner cities, universities, more exposure of school textbooks, of force fed Hollywood Democrat issues to their fullest. If they want MY issues or if they want condoms in schools, if they want inner cities, public schools, manufacturing, then get a law allowing to have kids have sex at home! I think the future is going to be awful! Like universities, unions, black churches,

[should we stop looking?]

What do you think: MORE attacks against Democrats, or allowing to have kids have sex at school, open ERs and hospitals!

[looking for what?]

Rather than try harder to reach you, in reaching you such, if your heart

God, if your heart shows up late,

I showed up almost two hours late and surprised everyone. The string of ancestors in my wake was singing to me a song I could hear through my shoes. Their names were floating inside them and seemed to filter something from their voices. Surprise, I said, I'm late. Sunshine was all around. Thick metallic sunshine.

I showed up almost two hours late and surprised everyone, Surprise! I said, I brought beer and all the great books and television shows, I'll show, I show you what it means to be surprised. I mean really surprised!

I surprised myself two hours late and surprised everyone. And feeling surprised I woke to all the websites and all the television shows, and what the sun looks like on television. Like, whoah! Surprise, God!

And in the matter of broken hearts, divinity. No, Serenity.

And in the matter of broken hearts, let's get better and try harder and erase all the things that we find only in ourselves.

I write to you with love in my heart and hand and my eyes and my teeth in my hand and my heart in my mouth bleeding down my face.

Dear God,

I appreciate your movies, and then appreciated them again. Folding one film inside the next I came to know you, and I came to love you, and I came to write to you, with my mind and my hands handshaking to do so. I don't think I'm important, and I don't resent that you are.

I know a lot of people think the world's already a wasteland, and there are others pretty convinced it'll soon become one. Every generation of Christians since Jesus has thought the Second Coming was going to happen to them. Your charm is staying classy in the face of despair. It's a indulgence in style for just the joy of being beautiful, God, beautiful God, call me information.

I know so much, I appreciate so much. There are spaces between people that can never be crossed: do I tell someone about this or not? The question, "Do I tell someone about this or not?" that is under every second of thought from the two very first brain cells snapping in our embryo to the thought that has us forget our voice and our sight, this question cannot be fully reported.

And I don't fully understand charity, though I receive it. If there is a thing that cannot be given, there are two things, and there are three of these things and from 3 come all things. When you give to me of yourself, she said, give me your face but not the muscle behind it.

Perhaps it is fate that today is the Fourth of July,
and inevitable in the course of history.

And once again you are fighting for your freedom,
to live, to exist.

In less than an hour, you will die.
Perhaps it's fate that today you shall die,

that you will lose, and that it's today
we should meet,

and like this.
We're going to live on,

but not you, America,
no part of you will.

Your endless seashores, mountains, etc.
will die, all of your skies,

all your flags.
America,

they'd rather live underwater and drown
than put up with more of your ecstasy.

The endless roads all end in the sea,
as surely as the rats do.

America, mute informant
of the pulse of the goat, America,

the slowest surgery,
the flowering land of God,

I eat all your words
and turn your children into knives.

"In one version of the game," "No referee in no other sport was so able to do so right by a game," "the winner sits the next round out. In another, the winner chooses the next winner." "while remaining so completely anonymous to his audience." "**Q**: When does a game stop being a game? At what level of importance?" "The Sport with the Most Organized Judicial System" "and in another, the winner is never revealed." "You must defend your house, and you get a gun to do this." "There's a good reason games have rules and judges—why there's so much fun to be had in the world bisected by limits." "Joining the referees is joining a team." "So much comfort, too." "Their job is to remain professional in an emotionally charged situation." "**A**: When it can refuse to stop being played." "One side is 'shirts' and the other is 'skins.'" "Something as specific as the pass interference rule becoming common knowledge." "To do so, they must learn to trust each other, and accept each others' judgments." "He was born in Detroit Mercy Hospital, and was a die-hard Detroit fan his entire life." "If a referee suspects another referee of taking sides," "He wed at twenty-four, and she bore him three sons." "Before the game, everybody's mind is on the game." "As if magnetized by the plural object," "they will speak privately after the game," "The rules of a joke are like the rules of a game:" The baby is pretending to be an egg, but it takes a mother to notice that. "There's the baby," the mother and father notice, "and only in the most extreme cases will the league be notified." "pretending to be an egg/soccerball." "You guys be skins." "When I was a child, I spake as a child," "there's the starting position/set-up," "I felt as a child, and I thought as a child." "the development of that position," "But when I became a egg," "No you guys be skins." "and various opportunities for reversals." "I put away childish things, was fertilized, died, and was buried, and grew up into a chicken dinner." "So the game ends, and each player thinks they lost. In reality, one of them didn't." "No,

you are skin / and I have lost," you finally understood. In the way the sky makes sense from the first time, your mind was big, glossy pages describing a pop phenom nee designer scent feedback loop and then, Oh Yeah!: you're a fundamental part of the national imagination now, now they know who you are. "I knew she'd be famous since the second she was born, but I never thought for what."

They were all guilty, and thankfully, all apprehended.

It would be a shame for anyone to go unpunished,

but thankfully, we all get it.

The inaccurate echo

Be in the way the description of glittering will sometimes cause it.
You will step into the chamber, hold on to the support bar, and while
stretched across the bardo of auditory hallucinations after the moment
of death. One of us says the lights and the other shatters them. Steps into
the chamber, puts on the headphones, the reflection of the whammy bar.
The way you talk about me to me.

Unquote echo

You find some new fortune in between the light's curve and blinking. Corporeal, edged, acoustic. Tied up to the bedposts, the way I use your eyelids is like it just occurred to us to ask us, want to have a kid together? But what can you use them for but suffering. Shelter them. Holocene. Ellipses in eclipse, the stars are all the Story of Fire. The way / you rise to work / and/or / every night, in person or apart, I know we'll fall asleep together.

In those moments that feel inexact, as when just out of sleep you turn around and fall back through the mirror, when you open your eyes to watch yourself open your eyes and the warmth of the bed feels like a record melting over your face in slow-mo sunlight in late June, and suddenly you really want to breathe, like then, in those moments

/

In those moments that feel inexact, when you feel the signature of another star on your particular estate, you can almost, in that habitat of foreign space/time, feel another god clawing its way from deep inside your mineral through your lungs and throat, as when reading words out loud you really mean but did not write

/

In those moments that feel inexact even the skin lining your shape, even your mind, mine, is the dumb drift of breath across wind, across the window, across your bedsheets and the seams of your headspace, and as you thrum with the echoes of my word, a reflection pinball through the architecture, refracting through the exact same noise

/

She notices you noticing her. You notice this, like normal, but then you notice something new: she knows how you think. What you're thinking. No. The nameless machines of your thoughts, she knows them as intimately as you do.

Yes. It's sudden.

The scenery is just sitting there like always, and the light is no different, splashed down the walls of the buildings to the concrete, and the people scattered about seem not to be aware that something is happening, and she's somehow developed in every wrinkle of the inside of your head. But not an image of her. Her herself. That's her over there inside of here. And it took no time at all.

These are her thoughts too.

You find yourself all over her head, riding the synapses of her vision, feel the lick of her eyelid across it, and you recognize the expression on your face from her eyes, and you've seen that somewhere, just a second ago, on someone else's face.

/


The heat of her tongue seals your eyelids, but her saliva sinks in anyways, something about it does. Your eyelashes and skin cells filter the liquid out of it, the taste of her taste, take away the saliva itself. Her meaning of it arrives in your vision ultra pure.

It's not what you hoped. What you hoped was so much smaller, provincial, ridiculous. What you hoped was washed away by when the first drops hit the cortex. What she means has nothing anymore to do with hope. The city of her experience spreads out before you, unfolds into more folds into street leading into alley into doorway into bedroom by bedroom by bedroom.

/


Morning reveals itself ripple by ripple,
sheds lovers and cities petal by petal.
A thin sheet covers her legs.
Soon, her vision fills the room.

/

Excerpt from *Eyelid Lick*
DONALD DUNBAR

for Rachel especially


for pleasant animals and warm plants


for prayers to angels, eternal gardens of feathers


for all the audio tape inside the earth, tangling like roots


for ten thousand dollars you would swallow this book and what else


for creosote, gasoline, drive-shifter, gasoline, chlorine, drive-shafts, wooden doilies, chamomile, gasoline, grenadine, sheaves of doves, creosote, gasoline, and wood-oil

for I remember the second time I recited the poem to you
for I remembered the children-voices I was going to do
for intimacy is inherently sudden

for Abby
for Allyson Alyssa for Phoebe and Andrea for Melanie for Julia Linda Leslie Christina and Trinka, for Nico, forgot Margaret but, ultimately, for everyone, really, this is all our doing, running in a fog of saturate light, in love, in emulsion, in love, in situ, in kif and in keeping with the thought of the mix, in thigh-high socks, in twelve-by-twelve pixel blocks breaking like breakdowns in likable

foreign pop, in Tame Impala, in alpha thru amygdala and on to in media res, pink cotton etceteras, etcetera, from the humble drum machine, from graveyard surcharges, from learned apes, an endless phonecall, from an endless phonecall, a signals marinade,
        from the sweetness of the initial comes the calorie of the name,
           for I arrived three hours late and surprised everyone of my dreams, my diagram, my chemistry, from my canonical accomplishments to Crater Lake, Oregon, Maddelyn High and I at The Farm Cafe and Farm and I at The Saz in Madison eating hummus and feta,
             for foods, etc., and for the sake of universal justice I dedicate this to you, eternal justice and food, "I parade in my parade costume," a love-letter italicized, forever and ever, for from the fashion of your vision comes the manner of your face,

            for the time you said capital-d Delighted: a promise to think about it until I'm dead
        from graveyards come funerals, come find out with me,

in-depth audience interviews administered bi-monthly
for from wet noise comes tea leaf bound into folio,
it is a gift of time we give inherently, actively, ceaselessly, mom, gosh,
for al-Abracadabra, alpha-beta, for to be afraid of
illegal love, instead, I live as a nun and a martyr:
from sunrise unto sunspot and belly-up again in
holy dawn, prayer daily restored, virginal, polite, apolitical as far as
economics and in love with the slim figures come through my window,
early morning familiars, when the mission bells come

within the air itself, undilated yet fully full air
with bells, bells, silver bells, sudden bells
increasingly soggy over hours and then years one
null
note over and ever and under and over again
additionally

increasingly loud, admittedly mass-produced, come in, come in,

it is amazing out there—

for I am Leviticus or one of the others

for I am alive to prove it

for I love the fragrance for its neck, and the stem for its vein

for I need no shield
for I need no shield

for I need to walk eighty ways and back
thru each scale
and to name each note its position to the
sun / and the sum / of earth's accomplished / spin
for when I lose myself I make damn sure
it was something I needed
for the insurgents in the good book:

a new end:

they want / no armor

# Interview

Where and when were you when drafting the first set of Clive Owen    I
poems? What time of day. What were you eating and drinking and
smoking? With pen and paper or on computer?

Can you explain how this acid trip clarified things for you around the    II
time of beginning these poems a little more? How did the experience
relate to your writing? What became clear? Would you go a little further
to connect the experience to the creation of these poems?

## Writing & Revising *Eyelid Lick*

# Donald Dunbar:

In September 2009 I was living at 3968 Mall St., Portland, Oregon in a 1920's craftsman house with four roommates. I was working at a professional college that wasn't paying me very much for a lot of time and energy. I was buying a vegetable I had never cooked each time I went to the grocery store and getting my friend Joel Brock to tell me how to cook it. I had recently had an acid trip that really clarified things for me, and was smoking weed and cigarettes er'ry day, drinking a couple of pots of tea and a few cups of coffee, and listening to a lot of music through a pair of Grado SR-60 headphones. I was using a laptop that would immediately turn off every time the cord got jostled.

I was writing at night during the week and spending most of the weekend writing too. I didn't have much of a social life at the time, and my roommates were all really interesting people so I mostly didn't have to go seek one.

I've learned a lot from doing a bunch of different psychedelics at a bunch of different points in my life, and I feel like everything I learn from anything relates to my writing. That trip in particular, though, was the first time I "found" the "Void". I don't know how else to put that.

Functionally, that trip gave me a lucidity within who I am and what the world is to me that I hadn't experienced before, however many places I looked for it. It shouldn't have felt totally by surprise—a lot of the ways I metaphorized the experience are more developed versions of ways I was thinking about myself just before—but it did.

Time is a big thing for me, and certainly doing any kind of drug is going to inform one's understanding of time. Meaning is another central thing, and I do think spending time with psychedelics would fundamentally improve 90% of people's understanding of this, ICP fanbase thru academia.

But that experience, out of all the times I've taken psychedelics, gave me the feeling not just of interconnectedness with the world, but of some huge oblivion chomping through every argument I could form and every hope and despair I could imagine. It felt great!

It also dislodged me and my writing from a lot of places I didn't realize they were stuck. I found it a lot easier not to worry what people think of

EDITORS:

Where did Clive Owen come from?  III  ----

Did you write for the sounds and rhythms or content?  IV  ----

The first batch reads more politically influenced than communicationally  V  ----
influenced. Were you experiencing much politicized content? Did these
stem from something political?

The final versions seem much more concerned with communication, the  VI  ----
issues of communicating one's ideas, perhaps the issues of the form of
poetry, or the form of speech and ways in which we communicate love
physically and verbally. Did you notice a shift in the theme from politics to
communication? Did you sense a theme at all developing, or were these
poems of sound?

# Donald Dunbar:

me—after all, won't we all soon be dead, and all the people we know, and all the things we've all done, in public or in private? And aren't all the various and detailed stories we invent for ourselves meant, in some way, to hide just that fact?

I think this is all easy to rationally comprehend, but I hadn't felt it for real, or felt really happy about it, before.

I was like, "Who's a person?" And then I was like, "Clive Owen."

Rhythms probably. But most of the things that got added in and stuck around are things that I didn't write "for" anything, even while I was doing it. I'm not totally against intention or anything, I've written pieces for people, for publications, for masturbation, for grades, for whatever, and I regret none of it. But something that I find more and more as this whole thing goes on is I end up cherishing the poems that had no thought towards their eventual use much more than I even look at the swarms of my poems that were, say, to prove I was good at writing poems.

Well, in 2009 politics couldn't be avoided, especially by a guy limited by money most nights to his computer. The Tea Party and Sarah Palin especially, but that summer I was really feeling duped into having voted for Barack Obama, and feeling really hopeless about all the grand things I thought people would figure out together.

The movement in this sequence probably traces in some way my political feelings over the period of revision. Rather than calling out the authority that be on how it's screwing everything up, I began thinking the only real way to supplant authority is to get all these hijacked brains to start practicing at interfacing with each other more deeply outside the models fed to them. This helped me unify my main streams of thought—poetry, politics, teaching, communion.

I didn't consciously notice a shift in the manuscript then, though later I saw a lot more fragmentation, poems slipping off into other documents or segments falling away. But I always had a view of the negative space. I write a lot, and lots of things—from automatic writings to one-off poems and who knows what else—don't make it into one of the manuscripts I focus most of my attention on, and I always have some idea of why they don't. Plenty of it is just garbage/practice/mapping, and some of it is stuff

The structure of these poems vary tremendously from one to the next,     VII
and sometimes morph within themselves. Many of them read like
letters or prose. Obviously your initial impetus was epistolary, but how
conscious of form were you when you began and when you revised? Is
there a scaffolding under all this? Is it intuitive for each poem, or are you
building a larger framework throughout the series with form?

How much time did you spend on the first batch?     VIII

How much time elapsed between creating the first batch and revising,     IX
and then how much time revising?

# Donald Dunbar:

I could probably get to *do* something but it isn't in line with what I really feel I've got to do/am doing.

Probably the most surprising shift in the manuscript was how the initially very ironic love slowly got revised into a representation of the real thing. I think this mirrors a shift in my headspace too, and I think it's related to the shift from politics to communication.

I was trying to imitate some aspects of a few different albums: *Ashes Grammar* by A Sunny Day in Glasgow, *Skoda Mluvit* by Schneider TM, and *Worn Copy* by Ariel Pink. All of these albums are really textural: Skoda Mluvit has like 500 different timbres of every grain in any song, or all of a sudden one pure shape; *Worn Copy* is the start of Ariel Pink's investigation into recording technologies and spaces and is melted and stepped-on; *Ashes Grammar* is the biggest headphone treat I have ever found, and one of the most beautifully choreographed documents I've ever experienced.

So much of what I was thinking about writing right then was translating what I felt very newly about music into poems, or translating poems into other textual forms. Growing up, music was mostly background noise or a group-identification mechanism, and it was only when I lived by myself in the cabin in the Upper Peninsula of Michigan for a few months that I started listening closely. Having that other form of art to play with ideas in / steal ideas from was really helpful in finding freedom in poetry. Whole bonus levels got unlocked very easily, things I couldn't have thought up by myself.

Not much. Like a few hours on each, a week or so for all of them. There was no quality control—I was writing them to amuse my roommates and because I had gotten to points in my other projects that were not fun at all. I'd collage a bunch of shit from online and stick it together in different ways and grab lines from my automatic writing and from the conversation often happening in the dining room and kitchen, where I was writing. And then I'd read them to whoever was around.

After writing the initial letters it was about two and a half months before my friend Ryan Donaldson, who's not a poet but who likes poetry, read them and suggested relaxing the boundaries between them, letting the form of the letter get a little wonky. It was early December 2009 I first started blending them, and the last revisions I made to them without the guidance of Rebecca Wolff were in November 2011—basically real

EDITORS:

These are part of a larger work. When and how did you realize these were
meant for the larger book? How did you decide where they belonged
(toward the end/climax of the book)?   X

I laughed out loud several times during these poems. Many more times   XI
in the final version. It caught me by surprise that I would be laughing, but
the surprise augments the hilarity I found in certain turns: "He emerged
from the closet the absolute picture of clothing." Do you find these
humorous? Certainly, the first batch is at least ironic, with its address to
an insignificant celebrity and such powerful and then absurd questions
and statements.

There are not that many visceral sensory details, like detailing the scenes,   XII
sounds, touches, smells, etc., but I definitely noticed when I encountered
them: "You begin to feel another set of eyelids close over your own..." is
a good example of strong sensory detail. This line follows some of the

# Donald Dunbar:

tiny detail tweaking at that point... like real, real miniscule. But I was reading the whole manuscript probably ten times a week for two years, and always thinking about each thing that was in there—that I could notice right then—for its relationship to the rest. And I always saved new copies of the document so in case I got stuck I could go back and start from another point.

I grew what became *Eyelid Lick* (nee *Tape decay*) around this/these poems, copying early drafts of the rest of the matter for the book into a whole-manuscript document. As soon as I started blending the poems together I knew I had to figure this shit out.

I was mostly totally bored of individual poems, but had recently read and loved John Beer's *The Wasteland and Other Poems*, Jesse Ball's *The Way Through Doors*, and reread *Sayonara, Gangsters* by Genichiro Takahashi, all of which play with the commerce between discrete parts. I was listening to album-albums, things you've got to listen to all the way through, and I'm not sure I could have tolerated another attempt at arranging individual poems, with their particular little signatures, after the months I had been at that.

I'm surprised now to see, as I'm looking through my folders to answer this, that although a bunch of pages were cut from the manuscript as a whole, enough to fill another book, only five pages were cut from the eventual version of this section. Lots of words were replaced, lots of things truncated and bred together, but my brutality wasn't full-on murderous with this.

I laugh at different parts of these a lot. I'm never like "Haw haw haw! I'm so funny!" except if I'm being weird, but I'll be like "You fucking guy!" and laugh and shake my head. I think most of the humor for anyone else probably comes from the words themselves, but a lot of the humor I find while writing them is remembering things I've written in the past, or things I used to be or have recently become. When you're drinking with someone for the whole evening and you reference something said earlier it can be way hilarious, but someone who just walked in wouldn't know it.

I'm never really turned on by description, literally too. There are, I understand, plenty of people who are, but I'd usually rather see a picture of it, or hear the story of it, or smell it and taste it.

rare moments of detailed audio descriptions. These also aren't in the first batch -- how did the sensory snippets make their way in?

Did you purposely hold off on sensory details to highlight these, or were you not working with the senses as much as the communicability of languages?

I find these wildly imaginative, surprising in a delightful way, pleasing and creative — you have mentioned wanting to start a school for creativity, or at least a program in creativity. How do you define creativity? How would you suggest cultivating it?    XIII

You use a lot of white space. What do you hope happens in the white space? Silence? Echoing? Reflection?    XIV

# Donald Dunbar:

The faux-epiphanic poems everybody's always bummed about—here's a bird/ here's a flower/ I learned something/ or felt something deeply—still usually make their big move rhetorically, but they don't put the work in before they go off, and going off is still just one move out of countless.

I'm way more interested in figuring out new moves than describing meals I can't eat and people I can't hear or see or touch.

If you're going to change a thing I think a good place to start is seeing the larger structures of it and around it, and how they narrow down the swarming mess of particles and ideas and spirits and relations and everything into "that thing there." Obviously, no one understands anything, at least when "thing" is "a particular narrowed down instance existing in limitless contexts and sharing myriad similarities with myriad other things," anyone just sees a small part of anything from really one tiny vantage point. Acknowledging this—deliberately acknowledging this, that no matter how much you know about anything there's *so much* to discover—is a really helpful mindset to start investigating a thing nobody's thought of yet.

When I was a student I was obsessed with being smart, and knowing shit, and making sure other people saw me as a smart dude who knows shit. And my poems from that time are all very imitative and all very flashy and, to me, have few redeeming qualities—they were, at best, novel. I had such a narrow sense of who I was, and since meaning is subjective, the world formed to meet this sense. When I got over myself, and when I started listening harder, my poems and my thoughts got a whole lot better in a very short time. And I've seen a number of other people find this same kinda thing.

There are certain paths and axioms to take and look at while examining a problem that are generally pretty useful, and I think these can be taught, and that's a big part of what I hope to make money doing someday soon.

If I could teach a younger me something very practical about cultivating creativity, I'd tell him to structure his life (emotionally, nutritionally, geographically, etc. etc.) so that he could take joy from the practice of it. It's way tougher to be creative when you're depressed and eating frozen pizza in front of *Friends* reruns.

I always had massive difficulty understanding white space when I was a student, and the times I'd sit down with the notion of using it would usually end with a pretty mechanical-tasting poem. Eventually, it started

"Perhaps it is fate that today is the Fourth of July" seems the most formal XV
of the batch. I want to ask you how you came to arrange these poems as
you have -- why this poem at this moment in the book?

The "X O" page seems pointed. It is not in the first batch. Since the XVI
entire series seems to express an absurdity in trying to express oneself,
especially in the matters of love, the "X O" fits well. However, why did you
decide to give it its own entire page and arrange the letters on the page
as you did?

# Donald Dunbar:

happening by itself and it wasn't like "Oh, I should use white space," but "How do I make this feeling happen here?"

With this stuff, one of my earliest hopes for it was that it'd produce the sensation of listening to an out of control radio, or an album that slipped from song to song without any real announcement. The forms of text in it—letters, plays, comment cards, MUD descriptions, etc.—all ask for a certain amount of white space / positioning, but a lot of the other positioning stuff is to help a reader keep momentum through such a long piece.

That poem starts with the melted-vinyl version of the president's inspiring speech near the end of *Independence Day*, the movie about the plucky Will Smith blowing up aliens, but it's a very slow poem with a lot repetition, and a confident voice. As best as I can piece together my decision-making process:

I want to keep it slow at that point, partially because the preceding bits have been pretty hyper-kinetic, and partially because I don't want to overwhelm the penultimate echo-poems and slash-poems. Those go right before the end because they're dreamy and strange and sort of a palate cleanser before the dedication page, which is the most incantatory part of the book. The Fourth of July poem carries on the ridiculousness— the grandiosity, paranoia, violence—of the preceding stuff, but makes you stick to the left side of the page with its short-lined couplets, getting you to calm the fuck down before switching to a more earnest speaker. It wouldn't do to have the speaker of the very sincere dedication page confused with the cruelty of "2" who's getting interviewed by 1, even though both impulses are mine.

Something I'm usually reevaluating in my work is the levels of irony. Take any poem or page or line and probably the initial impulse that got me typing it now seems wrong to me a couple times over. For instance, the stuff preceding the "x" and the "o" used to feel like the same kind of irony as the "Hollywood Democrats" stuff, and so the x//o felt at one point like a big f//u from me to poetry. Later I felt like, holy shit, that x//o is so sincere, and like something I'm discovering in my life away from the computer. Now that it's in a book, and that book is called *Eyelid Lick*, the x//o feels like another little machine burying fireworks in the road.

For instance, saying "eyelid lick" out loud, I feel every time like I'm going to say it wrong and I never do. It also is a pretty visceral image, and I am used to people sort of withdrawing into their imaginations when I say it to them. I think you almost have to picture this very intimate, heightened

You mention the economy in both batches. Is money something often    XVII
on your mind or on your mind while writing these poems? You have
recommended food stamps to me after finding them helpful. What's the
deal with money and poetry? There seems a time-honored tradition of
poets being less than rich -- is it a necessity?

# Donald Dunbar:

sense of touch / warm and wet and flesh-colored world of that kind of lick. I like how x//o crawls off the page a little, makes you feel a little shitty for flipping past it. I imagine that some people who know that the sentiment is not for them maybe try and imagine whom I mean it for.

I'd tell anyone coming up in poetry, if you can, get food stamps and buy local. I had an awful diet living on my own until I finally swallowed my Catholic-guilt-times-Lutheran-self-reliance, and learning about food helped me so many ways.

Top 5:

5. Cooking real food improved my mood, clarified thought, etc.

4. Cooking gets me away from the internet regularly

3. People you cook with or for generally feel real warmly towards you

2. People think it's sexy, so it's good for self-confidence

1. You can be mostly assured you'll never starve to death

But unless a poet comes from money, or has made money earlier in their life, poverty seems like a reasonable expectation for someone who spends most of their time staring at words they've already written. For me, the getting to a space where poems can be written takes a lot of time itself, and what works one day doesn't work next week, but then it kinda works a couple weeks later, and then you remember it like two years later and get something totally new out of it… then after the thirty minutes to six hours it takes to reach that spot, you've actually got to write a thing, and bosses don't think "I stayed up all night to write a six-line poem" is really an excuse for why you suck at your job today.

# Exercise

## World Building Through Map Making

Writers are creative animals. We like to jump right in when we get a new idea without taking proper steps to consider what the new world looks like. One way to get to the typing faster is to create a map. When we visually see what the story location looks like on paper, we can begin to identify what's missing.

Let's say you're writing a story about a family that lives on a farm in the late 1800s. (Think *O Pioneers!* by Willa Cather.) Your main character works in town, two miles from the farm. If you were to make a map, you would immediately mark these two locations. But what else is there? What surrounds the farm? What might your character encounter on that two mile journey?

Some questions you might ask yourself are:

Are there government buildings, like a sheriff, court, prison, a post office?

What natural features are present? Are there forests or lakes, rivers, hills, prairies, mountains, and so forth?

What stores might be in the vicinity? What other services are available, like a barber, smoke shop, bank, restaurants, and so on?

Are there places of worship?

What does the neighborhood look like? Who are the neighbors?

What historical events have happened in the area? Do any famous people live nearby?

What seasonal events might take place in this area? Is there an annual fair that people come from miles to go to?

What wildlife live in the area?

The key is to see your world from every angle. Even if your setting is only in one room, or a single building, you might consider what is beyond the four walls.

# Submitted by Hunter Liguore

Exercise:

Make a map of your world. Start with the most obvious features. In the above example it would be the farm and nearby town. Now look at all the open space. What can you add in those bare spots to make your town more real?

Here are some ideas: Library

Water tower

Prison

Ball field

Natural preserve

Carnival

Historic monument

What you add determines the outcome of your world. For instance, if you add a carnival to your world, the characters will probably attend, or at the least, discuss it. The goal is not necessarily to add details randomly, but to enhance your overall setting. In doing so, you have the opportunity to create a unique world, one that you can now navigate with ease.

Creating a map every time you start a story will allow you to fully imagine and then create this new world. When you go to lay down those details in the story, they will no longer be vague. "The library's over the next hill," becomes, "The library sat adjacent to the town's water tower, next to the dirt trail that runs past the sheriff's office." The more detail you can provide, the better your readers will see and appreciate the world you've created.

# Contributors

**Alicia Erian** has published a short story collection, *The Brutal Language of Love*, and a novel, *Towelhead*, which was made into a movie by Alan Ball in 2008. She was the Newhouse Visiting Professor of Creative Writing at Wellesley College from 2004-2008 and currently teaches at Northeastern Illinois University in Chicago.

**Donald Dunbar** lives in Portland, Oregon, and helps run If Not For Kidnap, a reading series and maker of small things. His first book, *Eyelid Lick*, won the 2012 Fence Modern Poets Series. He's published two chapbooks, *Click Click* (Gold Wake Press 2010) and *You Are So Pretty* (Scantily Clad Press 2009), and a third is forthcoming from Mammoth Editions at the beginning of 2013.

**Nicole Handel** Brooklyn-based artist Nicole Handel's work reflects inspirations drawn from the vibrant community of her adopted hometown of Bed-Stuy Brooklyn. Vibrant watercolor paintings juxtapose abstract illustrations with realistic images, the architectural precision of urbanity intersecting the dreamlike world of the imagination. Raised in New England but residing in New York City, Handel integrates her pastoral background with the spatial constraints of the street scape in her work. The artist studied undergraduate drawing at Pratt Institute of Art and Design. Her work has been featured in exhibitions throughout New York, New Orleans and Massachusetts, including the Antenna Gallery, Greenpoint Gallery, Fountian Art Fair Miami, and currently at Yes Gallery in Brooklyn, as well as a recent feature in Ladygunn Magazine.

**Hunter Liguore** Exercise contributor. A Pushcart Prize nominee, Hunter Liguore earned a BA in History and a MFA in Creative Writing. Her "anomalous" work has appeared in *Bellevue Literary Review*, *The Writer's Chronicle*, *Mason Road*, *The MacGuffin*, *Strange Horizons*, *New Plains Review*, *Barely South Review*, *SLAB Literary*, *Rio Grande Review*, *r.kv.r.y Quarterly* and more. Her short story collection, *Red Barn People*, is now available. skytalewriter.com

—